Follow the Lemming

by Kiki Thorpe

illustrated by Robert Roper

Ready-to-Read

Simon Spotlight/Nickelodeon

New York   London   Toronto   Sydney   Singapore

Based on the TV series *The Wild Thornberrys*®
created by Klasky Csupo, Inc. as seen on Nickelodeon®

SIMON SPOTLIGHT
An imprint of Simon & Schuster Children's Publishing Division
1230 Avenue of the Americas
New York, New York 10020

Manufactured in the United States of America

First Edition
2 4 6 8 10 9 7 5 3 1

Library of Congress Cataloging-in-Publication Data
Thorpe, Kiki.
Follow the lemming / by Kiki Thorpe ; illustrated by Robert Roper.—
1st ed.
p. cm. — (Ready-to-read)
"The Wild Thornberrys."
Summary: In the Alaskan tundra, Eliza agrees to play follow the leader with a group
of lemmings, a decision that may expose her and the rest of her party to danger.
ISBN 0-689-83599-X (pbk.)
[1. Lemmings—Fiction. 2. Alaska—Fiction.] I. Roper, Robert (Robert C.),
ill. II. Title. III. Wild Thornberrys ready-to-read ; #5.
PZ7.T3974Fo 2001
[Fic]—dc21
00-041940

Discovery Facts

Lemmings are small, furry rodents that live in very cold places. They make tunnels and nests underground, even when the ground is frozen!

Legend has it that lemmings will follow each other anywhere, even into danger.

"Stop following me!" Debbie shouted.
"I am not following you!" Eliza shouted.
"Girls, what is wrong?" their mother,
Marianne, asked.

"Well, I am stuck in Alaska," Debbie snapped. "And my sister is following me around like a lemming."

"I am not following you around like a lemming," Eliza said. Then she asked, "What is a lemming?"

"A lemming is a small animal that lives in cold places," Nigel said. "Legend has it that they will follow each other anywhere."

"Anywhere?" Eliza asked.

"Yeah, anywhere," Debbie said. "They get in all kinds of trouble—just like you, Eliza!"

"Well, I am not a lemming," Eliza said.
"Come on, Darwin and Donnie. Let's go!"

"Where are we going?" Darwin asked.

"Let's walk to the river," Eliza said.

Right then Darwin saw something move.
"What was that?" he cried.

Eliza looked around. "I do not see anything," she said. She took a step. Suddenly Eliza fell right through the ground!

"It is a trap!" Darwin cried. "Do not worry, Eliza! Donnie will save you!"

Just then a little animal popped up from the ground. "You are standing in my house!" he said.

"I am sorry," Eliza said. "Who are you?"

"My name is Louie. I am a lemming," he said.

A lemming! Eliza was very excited. "I am Eliza," she said. "This is Donnie, and this is Darwin."

"Would you like to meet *my* friends?" Louie asked.

"I do not know, Eliza," Darwin whispered. "Your sister said lemmings get into trouble."

"It's okay. Louie seems nice," Eliza said. "Where do your friends live?" Eliza asked Louie.

Louie gave a whistle.

"Right here!" he answered.

HELLO!

they all said together.

"This is Lulu. She likes to do flips. . . ."

"This is Lance. He can balance a rock on his nose. . . ."

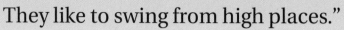

"And here are Lex, Lucy, and Lizzie.
They like to swing from high places."
"Hello," said Eliza.

"Want to play follow the leader with us?" asked Louie.

"I would love to play!" said Eliza.

"I do not think that's a good idea, Eliza," Darwin said. "Remember Debbie said that lemmings get into trouble?"

"Don't be silly, Darwin," said Eliza. "Let's play!"

"You can be the leader first," Louie said to Eliza.

"Okay," said Eliza. "Everyone stick out your tongue."

"Now hop on one foot," Eliza told them.

Z-Z-Z-Z

"Now spin in a circle," Eliza said.

"This is boring," said Louie. "It is my turn to be leader. Come on, everyone, follow me!"

Louie ran toward a cliff which led to a river . . .

. . . and jumped over the edge!

Suddenly all the lemmings
started running toward the river!

"Stop! You do not have to follow him!" cried Eliza.

But it was too late. One by one, the lemmings jumped into the river.

"Oh, no!" Eliza cried. She rushed to the river and saw . . .

. . . a swimming party?

"Come on in, Eliza! The water is great!"
Louie shouted.

"I guess you can not believe everything you hear. And I guess it is okay to follow the lemmings," Eliza said. "But I would still rather be a leader."

"Good! Then why don't you lead us home, Eliza?" said Darwin.

And she did.